Kim Fupz Aakeson and Niels Bo Bojesen

VITELLO
becomes a businessman

Translated by Ruth Garde

Pushkin Children's Books

The boy called Vitello lived with his mum in a terraced house right next to the ring road. He called his mum "Mum", and he called his annoying friends Max and Harry. He'd also got himself another friend, a little squirt called William. Vitello often ate spaghetti with grated cheese, and he liked scary films. Once he'd scratched his mum's car, but not on purpose, of course. Another time he'd bitten a postman on the leg, but he wasn't trying to hurt him. He wanted a dog and a dad, but of course you can't always get you want. He also watched quite a lot of TV. Today he and Mum were watching a programme about a boy who had already earned a million pounds, even though he hadn't turned eighteen.

"How much is a million pounds?" asked Vitello.

"A lot," said Mum.

"More than a thousand pounds?"

Pushkin Children's Books
71-75 Shelton Street
London WC2H 9JQ

Vitello Becomes a Businessman
Original Text: © Kim Fupz Aakeson and Gyldendal, 2008
Illustrations: © Niels Bo Bojesen and Gyldendal, 2008
English translation © Ruth Garde 2013
Published in the United Kingdom by agreement
with the Gyldendal Group Agency, Denmark

This edition published by Pushkin Children's Books in 2013

1 2 3 4 5 6 2015 2014 2013

ISBN 978-1-78269-001-6

Printed in China by WKT Co
www.pushkinpress.com

"Much more. Now be quiet."
"More than ten thousand pounds?"
"Shhh!" said Mum. "Much, much more."
"Damn!" said Vitello.
"Mind your language!" said Mum.

The boy on TV said, "I've always had a nose for business."

"Maybe I have too," said Vitello, and touched his nose.

"Ha!" said Mum. "I'll just be happy if you don't end up in the slammer!"

"What's the slammer?" asked Vitello, thinking that sounded even more fun than business.

"You've got plenty of time to find out," said Mum.

At the end, the boy said, "You just have to buy low and sell high."

That's good advice, thought Vitello, and rushed off to find his annoying friends Max and Harry and the little squirt William.

They weren't too keen on doing business. Max and Harry wanted to play with their stupid new Frisbee and William wanted to chuck stones at the ducks on the pond.

"No," said Vitello. "We're going to do what I say. We're going to do some business and earn loads of money. We'll make a million."

"A million? That's tons of money," said Max, or Harry.

"That's what I'm saying," said Vitello. "You just need to have a nose for it, and you have to buy low and sell high."

The others felt their noses.

Vitello said, "We just need to work out what we can buy low and sell high." Harry or Max suggested wild animals or sports cars. William suggested racing bikes. Vitello thought they should buy pistols, weapons and swords. Then they remembered that they didn't have any money to buy anything cheap. Not a penny.

"Let's go home and play with our new Frisbee," suggested Max and Harry.

"We'll think of something free that we can sell high," said Vitello. "That's even better."

But what was actually free? The boys thought long and hard. William said air. Max and Harry said earth. Then they couldn't really think of anything else. Then Vitello said, "Flowers. Flowers just grow out of the earth in people's gardens. And ladies love a nice bunch of flowers."

"But can we just take people's flowers?" asked William.

That boy asked so many questions.

"They'll grow again," said Vitello. "We'll pick them for free and sell them high and make a million. And before anyone even notices, the flowers we took will have grown back, and everyone will be happy, and we'll be even happier, and maybe we'll get on TV."

The brainy businessmen looked at each other, and agreed it wasn't such a bad idea after all. They strolled up and down in front of some terraced houses with flowers in the gardens, and found some quite pretty ones in rows of all different colours.

"Come on, businessmen," said Vitello. "We'll take those."

"Shouldn't we ask first?" said William. He really could be such a little squirt sometimes.

"I don't think there's anyone home," said Vitello, looking at the dark windows of the terraced houses. "You pick them. I'll keep watch."

William wanted to know how many they should pick. Vitello thought they should take all of them. "Otherwise we'll never be millionaires." So while Vitello kept watch on the house, the others took the whole lot. And there were enough for lots of bunches. In fact, they could barely carry all those flowers.

"We're not going to carry them. We've got to hurry up and sell them," said Vitello. "Let's get a move on."

The four businessmen started
with the posh houses. They rang the
doorbell of a complete and total
stranger and said, "How'd you like an
expensive bunch of flowers?"

The complete and total stranger said,
"I'm allergic. Flowers make me sneeze."

"These are very special flowers,"
said Vitello.

"AAAAACHOOOOO!!" said the man.

There was a boy who was at home
alone who couldn't care less about
flowers. There was a fat lady whose
sister owned a flower shop, so she
could get all the flowers she wanted.
There was a not-quite-so-fat lady who
said she preferred tulips. There was an
old man who couldn't hear what they
were saying.

And so it went on, from one house to the next.
They'd gone through the whole of the posh
neighbourhood and hadn't sold a single bunch.
    "We're going home to play with our new
Frisbee," said Max and Harry.

"No way," said Vitello. "The people living on those terraces like flowers more than the people in the posh houses. We'll be rolling in it."

It didn't look much like it. First there was one problem, then there was another. Everyone had an excuse for not buying any flowers. In fact, those flowers didn't look as pretty now as they did when they picked them. They'd started to look a bit droopy. But then they rang the doorbell of a sweet white-haired old lady who looked delightedly at their bouquets. "Ooooooh, dahlias!" said the sweet old lady.

"What?" said Max and Harry.

"The flowers. Dahlias. They're my favourites!"

"How about buying them for quite a lot of money?" asked Vitello.

"My garden is full of them," said the sweet old lady.

"I don't think so," said Vitello, looking round him. Then something or other crossed his mind.

"Oh, but it is," said the lady. "Just look."

"Where should we look?" asked William.

"Errr, we need to get going," whispered Vitello.

The sweet old lady pointed to her garden. Then she noticed that there weren't really any flowers at all where she was pointing. Not a single one. Her flowerbeds were completely bare and empty.

"But they were there this morning," she said.

Vitello gently tugged at the others' T-shirts.

"You can buy some new ones from us," said Max or Harry. The sweet old lady looked at their flowers. Then she looked at the garden, and back at the boys' flowers again. Then she shouted to her husband. "STAAAAAANLEYYYYY!"

"Let's get going," said Vitello.

The sweet white-haired old lady shouted, "STANLEY! THESE WRETCHED BRATS HAVE PICKED ALL MY DAHLIAS!"

"OK," said Max and Harry and William.

They didn't just get going; they RAN. Especially because the man the sweet old lady had called Stanley was running after them with a broom, which he was swinging over his head. Luckily the boys ran faster than Stanley, and in the end they got away.

"Phew!" said Vitello. "It's hard being a businessman."

"Especially the selling high bit," said Max or Harry.

"What are we going to do with all these flowers?" asked William.

"We'll sell them to my mum," said Vitello. "She's crazy about flowers and love and white wine."

"Cool!" said Max and Harry and William.

Mum was in the middle of doing the
hoovering when they got home.

"Hi," shouted Vitello, to make himself heard
over the hoover. "We've got some flowers
for you."

"Thanks!" shouted Mum. "They're gorgeous!"

"No, they're dahlias!" shouted William.

"We want some money for them," shouted
Vitello. "We're businessmen. We've got a nose
for it."

"You can have some squash," shouted
Mum, and turned the hoover off. The tired
businessmen looked at each other. "And a
biscuit," said Mum.

When the businessmen had had their squash and biscuits they lay on the grass, staring into space.

"We didn't make very much out of that," said William.

"We've probably got the wrong noses," said Max or Harry.

"We've got good legs, though," said Vitello.

"We got away from that Stanley and his broom, no problem," said Max or Harry.

"Exactly," said the boy called Vitello, who stretched and felt very pleased with his legs. He thought about all the places you could run to in the whole world. Luckily there were plenty to choose from.